D0519013

For Ava & Edward - S.P-H. xx

To Fin and Maia
Sebastien Braun

First published in Great Britain in 2015 by Boxer Books Limited.
www.boxerbooks.com

Boxer® is a registered trademark of Boxer Books Limited.

The illustrations were prepared using soft pencil and watercolour paint on hot press paper.
The text is set in Family Dog

ISBN 978-1-910126-55-4

1 3 5 7 9 10 8 6 4 2

Printed in China

All of our papers are sourced from managed forests and renewable resources.

Twit-to-Who?

Written by
Smriti Prasadam-Halls

Illustrated by
Sebastien Braun

Boxer Books

"Twit-to-woo," hoots the owl.
"Twit-to-woo!"
"Twit-to-woo?" says the sky.
"Twit to **WHO**?"

"To the animals at the farm, twit-to-woo.
Twit-to-QUACK, twit-to-BAA, twit-to-MOO!"

"Twit-to-woo," hoots the owl.
"Twit-to-woo!"

"Twit-to-woo?" toots the town.
"Twit to **WHO?**"

"To the bus and car and train,
twit-to-woo.
Twit-to-BEEP,
twit-to-HONK,
twit-to-CHOO!"

"Twit-to-woo," hoots the owl.
"Twit-to-woo!"
"Twit-to-woo?" sways the tree.
"Twit to WHO?"

"To the babies
in the bath,
twit-to-woo.

Twit-to-AHHH,
twit-to-OOH,
twit-to-COO!"

"Twit-to-woo," hoots the owl.
"Twit-to-woo!"
"Twit-to-woo?" says the house.
"Twit to WHO?"

"To the children playing games,
twit-to-woo.
Twit-to-hide,
twit-to-seek,
twit-to-BOO!"

"Twit-to-woo," hoots the owl.
"Twit-to-woo!"

"Twit-to-woo?" sighs the sun.
"Twit to **WHO?**"

"To the evening sky,
twit-to-woo.
Twit-to-pink,
twit-to-red,
twit-to-BLUE."

"Twit-to-woo,"
hoots the owl.
"Twit-to-woo!"
"Twit-to-woo?"
murmurs the moon.
"Twit to **WHO?**"

"To the world
going to sleep,
twit-to-woo.

Twit-to-me,
twit-to-them,
twit-to-YOU!"